Crick-Ette™

Written by Stephen Cosgrove
Illustrated by Charles Reasoner

READ ALOUD TOPSY-TURVY LIBRARY

H. S. STUTTMAN INC., *Publishers*
Westport, Connecticut 06889

READ ALOUD TOPSY-TURVY® LIBRARY
Published by H. S. STUTTMAN INC.
Westport, Connecticut 06880

PRINTED IN THE UNITED STATES OF AMERICA

ISBN 0-87475-600-6

8P(1586)40-444

A TOPSY-TURVY BOOK • A TOPSY-TURVY BOOK •

As you lay on a summer's day
In a warm and sunny place,
Don't look up into the skies;
Instead, look down
And squint your eyes.
Squint them both so very tight
That if you look
With all your might
You'll find the land of
Morethansmall.
And in this land are buggs,
that's all.

The wind whistled through the leaves of grass and among all the buildings of Bugg-ville. Even the hammers rang like musical bells, every nail they pounded.

Not far from Buggville, in a sheltered glen of clover trees, all the buggs came to sing or hum a tune, when work was done in the late afternoon. The music soared above the night and you could see a wondrous sight: A bugg on piano. A bugg on drum. Your feet started tapping and you had to hum.

THE
ALI-BUGG

Not far from the glen, sitting all alone in a mushroom grove, was a sad and lonely cricket named Crick-Ette. She sat on her stump and tried not to listen, but the music, the music was all she could hear.

Then Crick-Ette's tears, with a rhythm all their own, dripped and dropped from her eyes, to her fingers, to her toes.

For earlier that evening she had joined the other buggs as they sat around listening to a rousing good song. As everybugg joined in and sang the chorus, Crick-Ette, too, began to sing along. But the note she sang was so sour that mirrors cracked and giant dogs bayed at the moon.

She had rushed to the mushroom grove and sat all alone, too cold to stay, too embarrassed to leave. Finally, because there was no way she could stay out all night, she slowly headed for home.

Poor Crick-Ette! Her eyes brimmed with tears and all of the trail was nothing more than a blur. She stubbed her toe on a twig, tripped on a stone and stumbled over a sleeping caterpillar.

"Excuse me," said the caterpillar, perplexed and amused, "Who's tripping over me while I snooze?"

"It was me," said Crick-Ette, quite confused. "I didn't see you, lying there while you snoozed."

The old caterpillar stretched his many arms and yawned a deep and melodic yawn. “Ahhh! Little crickets should watch where they walk late at night,” he rumbled like a bass trombone.

“Oh, I am so sorry!” sobbed Crick-Ette. “I wasn’t paying attention. You see, the trouble is, I can’t sing. The music won’t sink into my head.”

“There, there,” the old caterpillar said, “You can’t make music with your head. You must make it with your heart instead.”

Crick-Ette's little cricket eyes lit up. "Of course," she thought. And she thanked the caterpillar and ran home to find a musical instrument that would express the music in her heart.

Bright and early the next morning Crick-Ette went out back, where the daisies grow, and tried every musical instrument she could find—the tuba, the oboe, even a rose petal horn. None of them was exactly right. They all sounded a lot better than her singing, but there was still something missing.

Crick-Ette thought and thought, and then she thought some more. “I’ve tried all the horns, but they just don’t seem to be right. I tried the piano and it wasn’t right. Hmmmm.”

Suddenly, she remembered that in the attic was her grandpa’s old violin. “I don’t need to dawdle or diddle. I can learn to play the fiddle!” With that she dashed up the stairs to the attic where the fiddle was stored.

TOYS

Crick-Ette dusted off the violin, put rosin on the bow, and then, like a wild bugg, she let it all go. She didn't play classical as she whirled around. The song she felt had a country sound.

Later that afternoon she slipped quietly back to the musical glen where everybugg was singing along. She didn't try to join in, but gently swayed with the beat.

Finally, some bugg asked, "Crick-Ette, can you play that fiddle?"

She smiled kind of shyly and said, "Well, just a little."

She walked to the stage, where she removed the violin from its case, tuned it very carefully and began to play.

With a whoop and a cheer all of the buggs began dancing with anybugg near.

. . . So, if you can't sing . . . and not everyone can . . . remember Crick-Ette and her All-Bugg Band!

A TOPSY-TURVY BOOK • A TOPSY-TURVY BOOK •

A TOPSY-TURVY BOOK • A TOPSY-TURVY BOOK •

If your father's a baker
Or just a garbage man, true
Think of this little story
Of a bugg named Cooty-Doo.

That very next day at school, when the buggs were at recess and the garbage wagon came rolling by, Cooty-Doo waved proudly at his dad as the other kids chanted their silly chant.

The other buggs looked on in disbelief as Cooty-Doo, with head held high and with a smile wider than wide, said, “That’s my old man! Best darn garbage man in the whole world!”

The two of them talked as they walked into the evening's hush. Litter Bugg taught Cooty-Doo that no matter what you do in life, there's always something better. And no matter what anybugg does there will always be somebugg who will make fun and not understand.

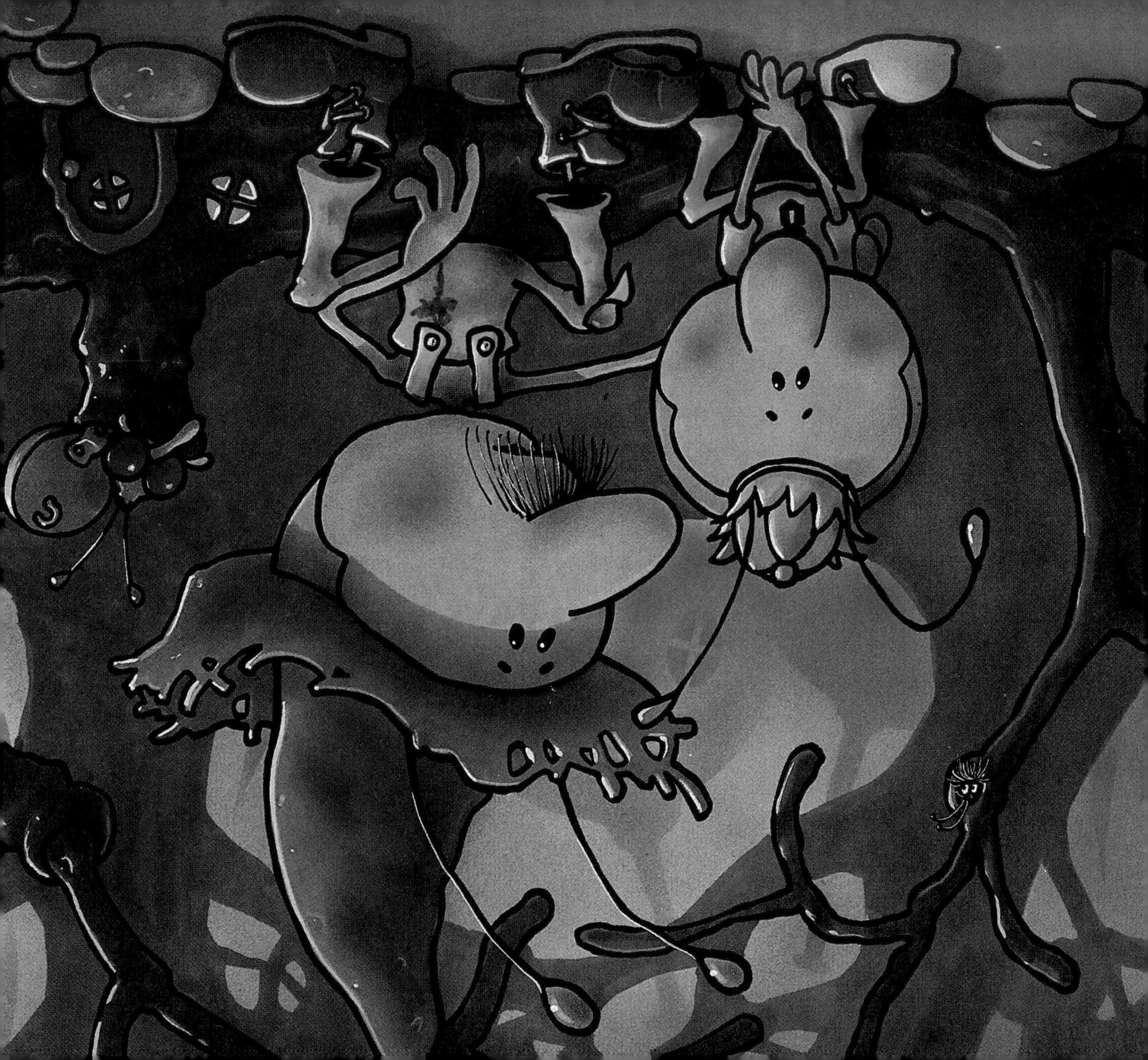

With hands between his knees, Cooty-Doo told his dad the whole story. He even told him that he chanted the junk-man song with the other buggs in the playground. “You see, dad, I want to bc proud of you, but you’re just the garbage man!” With that he once again broke into tears.

Old man Litter-Bugg put his arm around his son and said, “I could do something else. I could be a butcher or a baker or a lamplighter maker. But I like what I do. And what I do doesn’t make me any better or any worse than I already am.”

He ran and ran until he just ran out of breath and fell sobbing onto a pile of moss in a clearing. He lay there and cried and cried until a voice broke his reverie. “Hey-up! What seems to be the problem, little bugg?” Cooty wiped a blurry tear from his eye and looked around. There stood his dad.

"Yes, Cooty, I'm talking to you. Do you want a ride home or would you rather walk with your friends?"

Cooty-Doo was so embarrassed that he ran as fast as his little bugg legs would carry him into the clover forest.

Fortunately Cooty was saved by the class bell; as it rang he muttered, “Really neat stuff!”

Later, just as the school bell rang at the cnd of the class day and all the buggs escaped to home and play, the garbage wagon came creaking by again. To Cooty’s horror, his father stopped the wagon and asked his son if he wanted a ride. “Who? Me?” Cooty asked, “Are you talking to me?”

8

The wagon creaked by the playground. Litter Bugg, with a tear in his eye, pretended to ignore the shouts. Sad to say, right in the middle of the gaggle of giggling kids was Cooty-Doo, chanting louder than all the rest.

With the wagon gone and recess over the bugg kids filed back into school. "Hey, Cooty! What did you say your dad did?" Glance shouted out.

"Oh, uh, he's a . . ." Cooty sweated out an answer, "he owns his own business! A big business . . . making stuff!"

The other buggs became interested and Snugg asked, "What kind of stuff?"

So every morning he got up at the crack of dawn and sneaked into town so the other buggs wouldn't know where he lived.

At school none of the other student buggs knew what Cooty-Doo's dad did for a living. If anyone ever asked, Cooty would mumble this or that; usually, he avoided the question. One day on the playground the garbage wagon slowly rolled by and all the buggs laughed and chanted, "Garbage and junk. Stink and stunk. Litter Bugg smells like a dirty old skunk!"

OLD
BLUE

The Litter Bugg family wasn't large. It consisted of old man Litter Bugg, his wife Letty and their young son, Cooty-Doo. They lived in a small house at the edge of the dump so that old man Litter Bugg could be close to his work.

Because they lived near the dump, which was a far fly from town, Cooty-Doo had to walk a long way to get to Buttonwood School. He could have ridden with his father, but Cooty was ashamed of what his dad did and would rather walk than be seen on the garbage wagon.

LITTERBUGG
GARBAGE
CO.

It was here that Litter Bugg and his family lived. They were no different from the other buggs who lived in Buggville, except that they did a job nobody else wanted to do but that had to be done just the same. In the early morning's gloom Litter Bugg would drive his wagon on his appointed rounds to pick up the refuse that had to be thrown away.

BUGGVILLE
Dump
Enter

Before the buggs of Buggville even thought of crawling from under their warm dandelion-down quilts, the garbage wagon would make its way south out of town a mile or two, to a place where very few buggs went, let alone lived.

The wisps of mist dipped and danced around strange and menacing piles of rubber tires here, tin cans there, garbage, garbage everywhere. For, you see, this was the Buggville Dump.

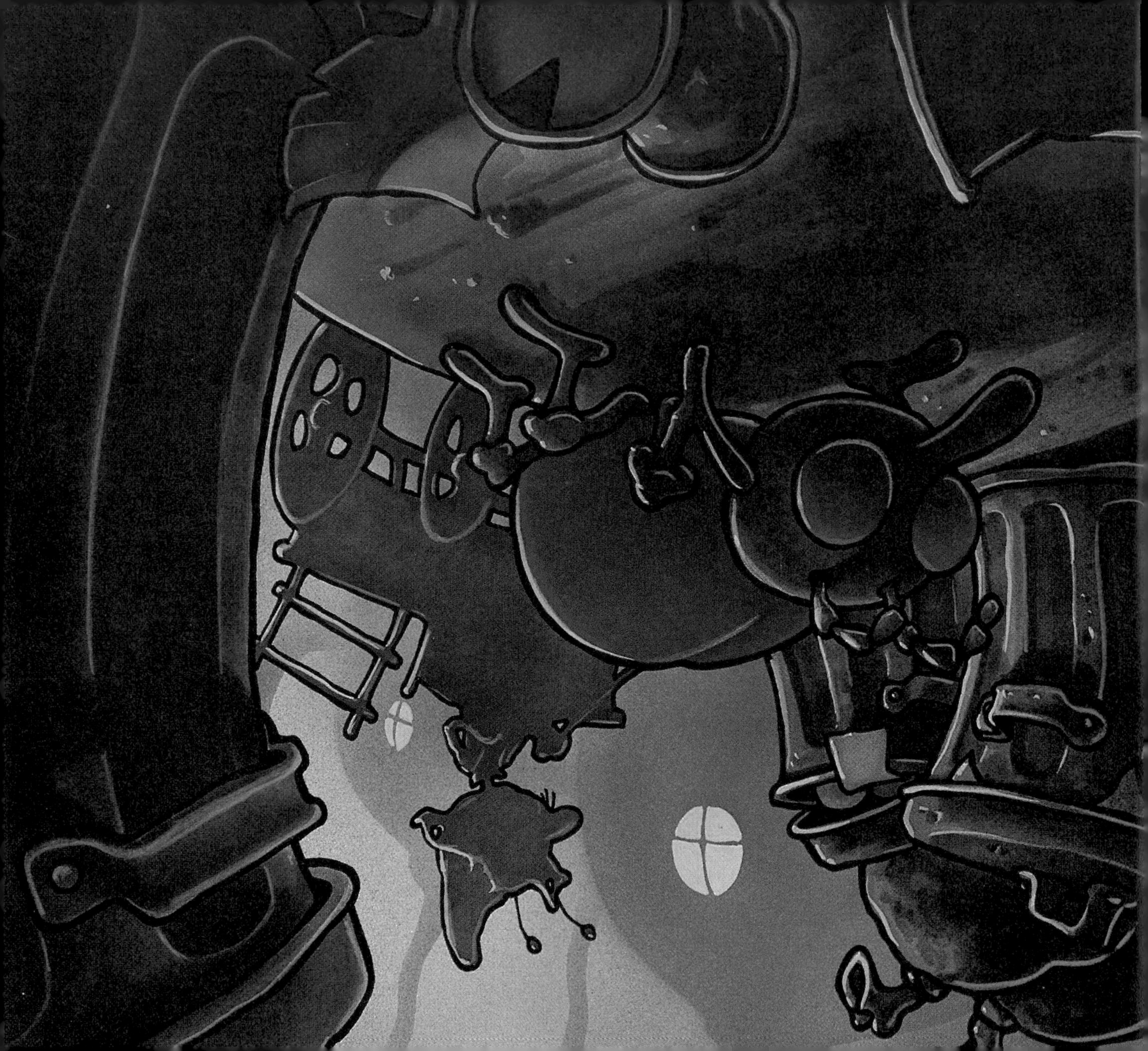

The streets of Buggville were always empty in the early morning dawn. It was a time when all the streets were damp and there was no sound save the occasional yip or yap from somebugg's pet bark bugg or the creaking of the clover tree. All quiet, no one awake, except a solitary figure driving a ramshackle, clanking wagon from house to house picking up the garbage placed outside the night before.

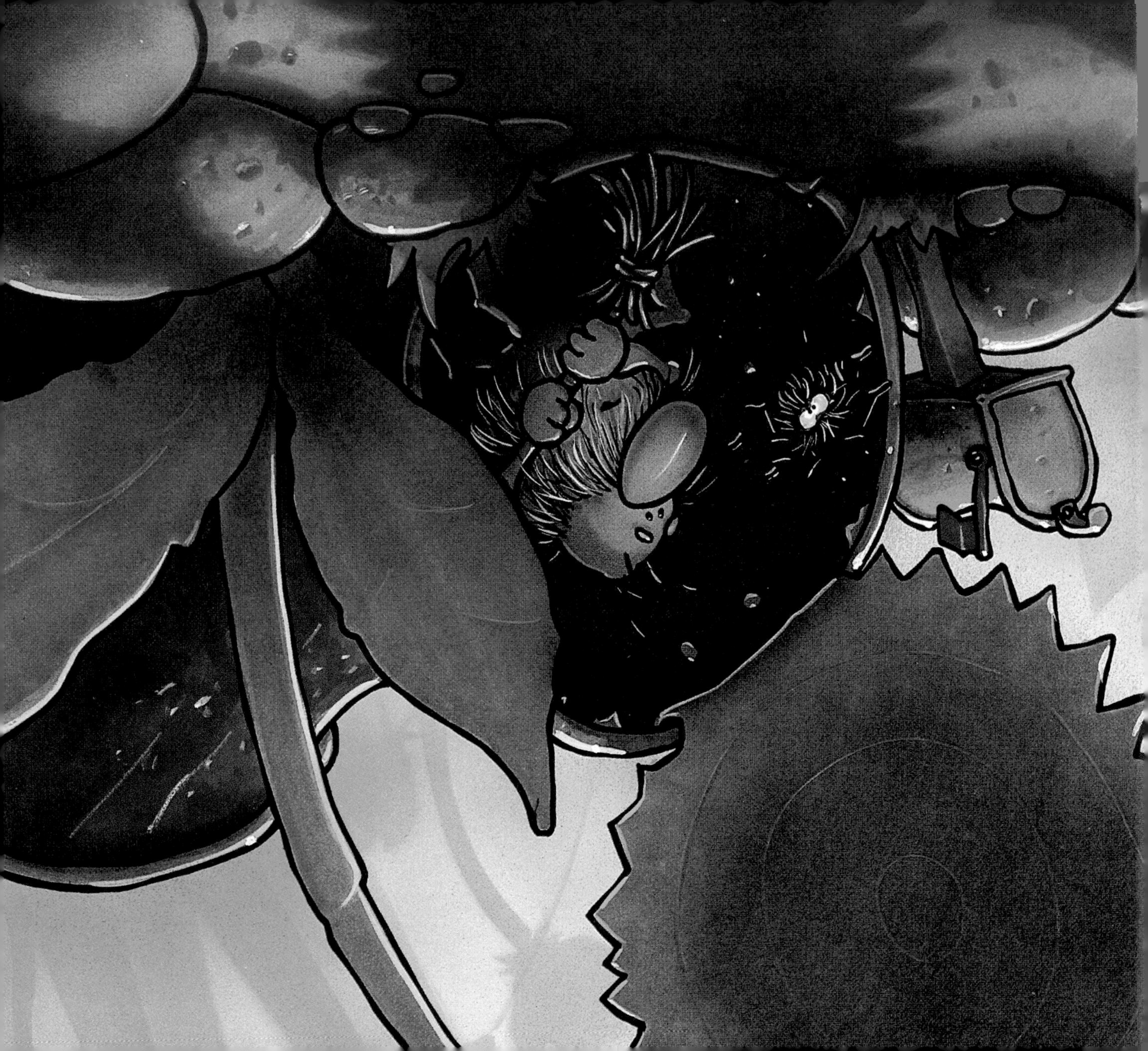

As you lay on a cool spring day
In a warm and sunny place,
Don't look up into the skies
Instead, look down
    And squint your eyes.
Squint your eyes so very tight
And if you look
    With all your might,
You'll find the land of
    Morethansmall.
For in this land live buggs,
    that's all.

A TOPSY-TURVY BOOK • A TOPSY-TURVY BOOK •

READ ALOUD TOPSY-TURVY® LIBRARY
Published by H. S. STUTTMAN INC.
Westport, Connecticut 06880

PRINTED IN THE UNITED STATES OF AMERICA

ISBN 0-87475-600-6

8P(1586)40-444

Cooty-Doo™

Written by Stephen Cosgrove
Illustrated by Charles Reasoner

READ ALOUD TOPSY-TURVY LIBRARY

H. S. STUTTMAN INC., *Publishers*
Westport, Connecticut 06889